This elephant baby
Gets treats from her mother.
Just open the flap,
And she'll get another.

The peacock struts proudly
In bright green and blue.
Now open the flap—
See what else it can do!

It looks like the monkeys
Might rest the whole day.
But just lift the flap,
And you'll see them at play.

Some say to beware of
This animal's grin.
If you open the flap,
He'll welcome you in.

This animal is tall,
Taller than a tree.
If you think we're kidding,
Lift the flap and see.

How do sea lions dine
With no hands and no feet?
Just open the flap,
And you'll see how they eat.

Animals look amazing,
And strange are the things they do.
But remember, to the animals,
We look amazing, too!